# PLANET FOOTBALL

## Michelle Robinson    illustrated by Chris Mould

WALKER BOOKS
AND SUBSIDIARIES
LONDON • BOSTON • SYDNEY • AUCKLAND

# Jackson loved football.

He loved it the best.

He never gave football the tiniest rest.

He played it.

He watched it.

He ate it.

He slept it.

His friends and his family came to accept it.

He learned all the players, the fixtures, the scores.
He played it inside and he played it outdoors.
And that's how it happened, one grey cloudy day,
when Jackson had taken his ball out to play...

He played all alone, unafraid of the thunder.

*How high can I kick it?*
he started to wonder.

He took a big run up,
he KICKED, and ...

# oh, my!
His football went flying right into the sky.

It flew through the wind
and it flew through the rain!

It flew through the clouds ...

and it just missed a plane!

It didn't stop there...

Jackson's ball kept on going.
Where would it stop?
There was no way of knowing!

A passing reporter said,
"Kid, you're tremendous!
That kick was astounding!
That kick was stupendous!
A ball up in space? You'll be famous for sure!"

And the next day he found ...

a huge crowd at his door.

"Show us your skills, Jackson. Kick it to Mars!"

Now he was one of the world's biggest stars.

He went to each country,

each city and town,

kicking footballs so high,

that they never came down.

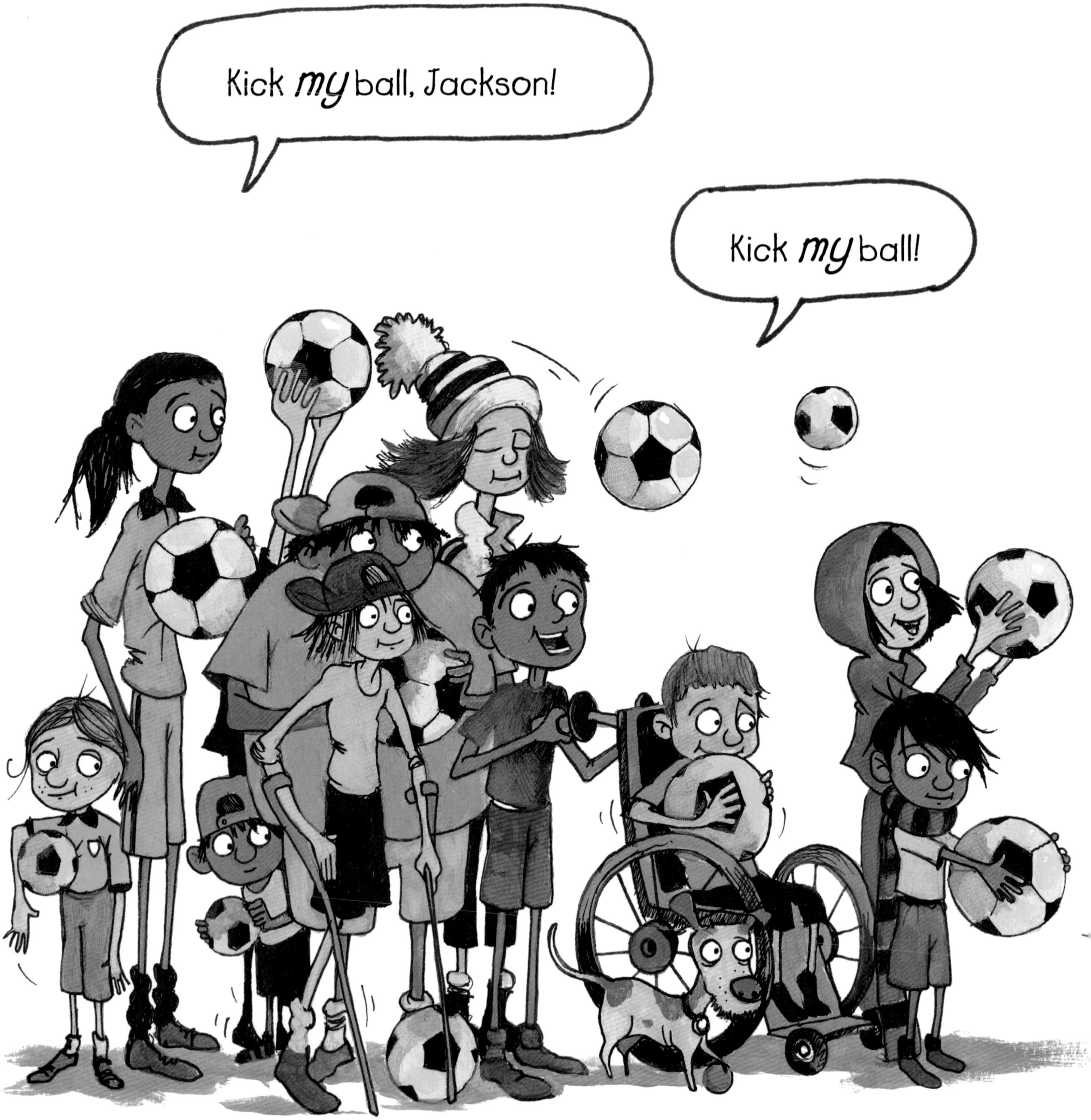

Kick *my* ball, Jackson!
Kick *my* ball!

And soon...

WERE STUCK ON THE MOON.

No balls left on Planet Earth?!
Jackson felt bad.

Meanwhile, the moon-folk had gone football mad.

But they'd not seen anyone play it before.

Instead of just ONE ball ...

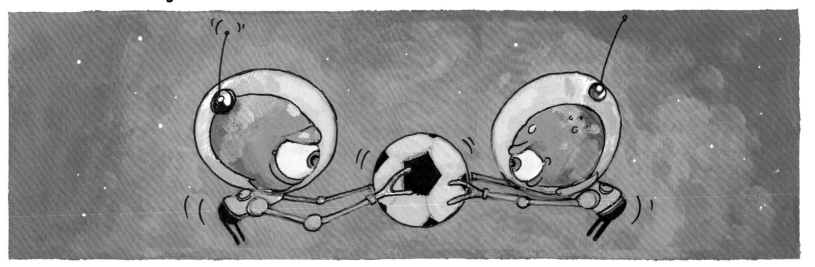

they each wanted MORE!

A star football player said, "What a to-do!
The World Cup's been cancelled now, all thanks to you."

They cancelled the World Cup?! He just couldn't bear it.
He'd only shown passion and wanted to share it.

"A world without football's a world without fun."
Jackson said, "I MUST fix this…"

"Come on, everyone!
If we're going to do this,
we need a whole team..."

Soon he and his buddies
were building up steam.

Jackson loved football.
He loved it the best!
His moon mission put
all his skills to the test:

captaining rocket ships,
taking his aim ...

the Earth's favourite game.

"Can we have our balls back? You only need one.
We've taught you the rules now – enjoy it! Have fun!"

He gave up his own ball – the moon people kept it.

They played it! They watched it! They ate it! They slept it!
They learned all the players, the fixtures, the scores.
They played it inside and they played it outdoors.

The World Cup was on again. Big relief! Phew!

An Out-Of-This-World Cup was played in space, too.

I'm sure you'll be thinking, *That can't happen, can it...?*

But who knows what's out there, beyond our home planet?

Take out a telescope.
Look with great care.
You might spot a pitch and
some goalposts up there.

It just takes one kid on a grey cloudy day.

So, go find some friends ...

throw a ball down ...

let's play!